THE PET STORE JOB

"I think this thief, whoever it is, is stealing my loose biscuits, too!" Mr. Burns complained. "They must be filling their pockets every time they come in!"

"Wouldn't you see them?" Liam asked.

"They're too clever for that!" Mr. Burns replied. He scooped some biscuits into the bag, weighed it, and handed it to Becky. "But next time, I'll be ready for them!"

Titles in Jenny Dale's POLICE PUP series

THE PET STORE JOB

Jenny Dale

Illustrated by Mick Reid

SCHOLASTIC INC.

New York Toronto London Auckland Sydney
Mexico City New Delhi Hong Kong Buenos Aires

Special thanks to Narinder Dhami

Many thanks also to
Steve Dean and Peter Whitehead
of the Metropolitan Police Service for their
valuable advice

In memory of a tiny copper-colored pup called Beulah,
who was rescued by a police officer
and grew up to be a very special dog

ISBN 0-439-32264-2

12 11 10 9 8 7 6 5 4 3 4 5 6/0

Printed in the U.S.A. 40

First Scholastic printing, November 2001

Chapter One

"Fetch, Max!" Liam Wilson hurled the ball as far as he could into the distance. "You, too, Scooter!"

"I don't think Scooter will beat Max!" Becky, Liam's twin sister, laughed as the two dogs shot off together across the park. Sure enough, Max's long, loping stride soon outran the little terrier's. He stopped the ball neatly, picked it up between his teeth, and raced back to Liam, his long, bushy tail wagging proudly. Scooter, meanwhile, trotted back, panting, his little pink tongue hanging out.

"Poor Scooter!" laughed Julie Gibbs, the twins' neighbor, as she scooped her dog up into her arms. "He never has a chance to get the ball with Max around!"

Liam grinned and looked at Max. "Stay, Max!" he said firmly.

Max sat down immediately on the grass on his powerful haunches, his dark eyes fixed on Liam. Even when Liam threw the ball across the park again, Max barely moved a muscle. This time Scooter scampered after it, picked it up, and bounded happily back to Julie.

"Good dog, Scooter!" Julie said. "Give me the ball now! Come on, good dog! SCOOTER!"

Scooter had obviously decided, now that he had the ball, that he wasn't go-

ing to give it up for anyone! He held onto it tightly and wouldn't let go.

Max, meanwhile, sat watching everything that was going on with interest, the breeze ruffling his thick brown-black coat. His tail wagged gently, and his long, pointed ears pricked upward, but still he didn't move.

"Come, Max!" Liam called, and Max immediately bounded over to join them.

"Oh, I wish Scooter was as well behaved as Max!" Julie sighed after finally managing to wrestle the ball out of the terrier's mouth.

"Well, Max has had special training!" Becky said proudly.

Although Max was the Wilson family's pet, he was also a highly trained police dog who worked with the twins' father, Officer Wilson, at the local police station. The Wilsons had moved to Ellandale in the Peak District of Derbyshire last summer so that Officer Wilson and Max could start their new job. Living in the country was very different from the city life Liam and Becky had left behind, but now neither of them wanted to live anywhere else.

"There's Dad." Becky waved as her father jogged past in the distance in his blue warm-up suit. Officer Wilson, a tall man with the same dark hair as Liam and Becky, waved back and continued on his run. He was serious about keeping fit, which had been useful a couple of weeks ago when he'd been drafted onto the Ellandale soccer team on short notice for an important game. The trophy that was to be presented to the winning team had been stolen, but Max had found it. Now Max's detective skills were famous in Ellandale.

"What are you going to do during vacation?" Julie asked as they went over to the swings, Max and Scooter jumping playfully around them.

"Play soccer!" Liam said instantly. School had closed the previous Friday for vacation, and although it was late autumn, the weather was still mild.

"Typical!" Becky laughed. Liam was crazy about soccer. "Don't forget we have book reports to do for Ms. Kendall before we go back."

Liam groaned. "I know, and —" He stopped as Max caught his attention.

The German shepherd had suddenly stiffened and was standing very still, ears cocked, staring beyond the swings at the bushes along the back of the playground.

Liam glanced over to where Max was staring but couldn't see anything. "Max, what is it?" he asked, puzzled.

A few seconds later, a large black-and-white dog came out of a hole in the bushes and trotted over to the swings. Max had realized the dog was there before anyone had been able to see him.

"Hello, boy!" Becky said. "I wonder

who he belongs to?" The dog seemed friendly enough — his tail was wagging.

Scooter had disappeared behind the trash cans to investigate a particularly enticing smell, but Max was still watching the black-and-white dog.

Liam knew that German shepherds were suspicious of anyone new, dogs or humans, but Max was generally all right with other dogs once he'd gotten to know them.

"I think he must belong to that family over there," Becky concluded as Max and the other dog sniffed each other cautiously.

"I don't think so," Julie pointed out. "They're going without him."

Sure enough, the family was leaving the playground and hadn't even glanced at the dog.

"Oh, well, maybe he belongs to one of the joggers," Becky said. "Look, he has a collar on."

Max and the dog had become cautious friends by now, and Becky got off her swing to pet them both. The black-and-white dog seemed pleased and licked Becky's fingers.

"I wonder if he's lost," Liam remarked.

"Maybe we should see if we can find his owner," Becky suggested.

At that moment, Scooter emerged from behind the trash cans. He spotted the black-and-white dog and, giving a friendly little bark, rushed straight toward it.

The strange dog's behavior suddenly changed. His ears went back and he bared his teeth, beginning to growl deep in his throat.

Scooter skidded to a stop, looking very scared. Then the other dog charged toward him, growling and snarling loudly.

Chapter Two

"Scooter!" Julie screamed, her face pale with horror. "SCOOTER!"

Liam and Becky both froze, too stunned to move. The dog had seemed so friendly toward them and Max. Who could have suspected that it would react like this when it laid eyes on Scooter?

Max immediately took charge of the situation. He ran ahead of the black-and-white dog, pushing his powerful body between it and the little terrier. Max stood his ground, growling faintly but menacingly, keeping the other dog at bay. Meanwhile, Scooter cowered behind Max, shivering and shaking.

Liam, Becky, and Julie watched, their hearts in their mouths, as Max and the black-and-white dog stood staring at each other. The black-and-white dog slowly began to back away.

"What's going on here?" asked a quiet voice behind them.

"Dad!" Becky gasped. She had never been so relieved to see her father before.

"That dog tried to attack Scooter!" Liam told his father in a low voice. "He was all right with us and with Max, but when he saw Scooter, he went for him!"

Officer Wilson squatted down and held out his hand to the black-and-white dog. "Hello, boy," he said in a calm, confident voice. "Where did you come from?"

The dog shot a last wary look at Max, then turned his attention to Officer Wilson. Slowly his tail began to wag, and he trotted over to sniff the policeman's hand.

Officer Wilson talked to him quietly for a few moments, then calmly pulled Max's leash out of his pants pocket and clipped it to the dog's collar. The dog had no objection.

"You can pick up Scooter now, Julie," Officer Wilson said.

Julie rushed over to her little terrier. "Scooter!" she gasped, grabbing the little dog. Scooter was shivering and still looked scared, very different from his usual mischievous self. "Thank goodness Max was here!"

"Yes, good boy, Max!" Liam, followed by Becky, hurried over to hug the German shepherd. If it hadn't been for Max, things could have gotten out of control.

Officer Wilson was reading the tag on the dog's collar. "His name's Monty, and there's an address here. I think we'd better see if his owners are in the park, and if not, we'll take him back to them."

"I'll take Scooter home," Julie said, hugging her dog tightly. "He's still upset." She reached out and ruffled the thick fur around Max's neck. "Thank you, Max," she said in a shaky voice. "You're a hero!"

"This is it." Officer Wilson stopped outside a house near Ellandale's main street. "Number five."

"I hope you're going to give Monty's owners a talking-to, Dad!" Liam grumbled as they led Max and Monty up the path to the front door. "They're not looking after him if he's roaming around on his own!"

"Well, I'm not officially on duty!" Officer Wilson's eyes twinkled as he rang the doorbell. "But let's hear what the story is first, okay?"

Becky grinned to herself. If it were up to Liam, he'd jump right in with the talking-to before he'd heard the owner's side of the story!

The door was opened a moment later by a young woman in jeans and a red sweater. "Yes?" she asked, looking puzzled. But before Officer Wilson was able to say anything, she suddenly spotted Monty and gave a little cry. "Monty! What on earth are you doing *there*?"

"I take it this *is* your dog?" Officer Wilson asked, raising his eyebrows.

Monty was going crazy, pawing at the woman's knees as she bent down to pet him.

"Yes, he is." The woman now sounded completely bewildered. "But what's he doing with you? He was in our backyard!"

"We found him in the park," Liam chimed in. "He was attacking our friend's Jack Russell!"

"Oh, dear." The woman looked embarrassed. "I'm afraid Monty just doesn't like small dogs. He's all right with bigger dogs, though, like your German shepherd there —" She stopped suddenly as if a thought had just struck her. "Is that the Ellandale police dog?"

Officer Wilson nodded. "Yes, that's Max, and I'm his handler, Officer Wilson, although, as you can see, I *was* off duty when Monty turned up!"

"Oh, no!" The woman turned almost as red as her sweater.

Becky began to feel sorry for her.

"You must think I'm an irresponsible dog owner, Officer Wilson," the woman went on. "But I really did think Monty was in the backyard. We *never* let him out on his own!"

"I'm sure you don't," Officer Wilson reassured her. "But perhaps I could have a quick look at your backyard. If Monty did escape, I may be able to suggest how you can make it more secure."

The woman, who introduced herself as Mrs. Reed, agreed immediately and led them through her house into the long backyard. It was very overgrown. The weeds were about a foot and a half high.

"We only moved in a few weeks ago," Mrs. Reed explained. "We haven't had a chance to do much with the yard yet."

"We can see that!" Becky whispered to Liam. "It's like a jungle!"

"Good thing they don't have a small dog," Liam whispered back. "They'd never find it in all these weeds!"

Officer Wilson looked around the whole yard. Beyond it was a wide alley that ran behind some of the stores on the main street and was used as a shortcut by local people. "That's probably the route Monty took to the park," he said. "But I can't see any obvious place where he could have gotten out," he added with a frown. "The fences and gate are a bit rickety, but there are no holes in them."

"Maybe Monty jumped over the gate, Dad," Liam suggested.

But Officer Wilson shook his head. "I know Monty's a pretty large dog, but it would still be too high for him. I wonder how he did it."

Chapter Three

"Mom, can we go to the pet store this morning?" Becky asked as she finished her cornflakes. "We want to buy a dog treat for Scooter."

"We think he deserves a nice surprise after yesterday!" Liam added. "He was pretty shaken up after Monty tried to attack him."

Becky and Liam were having breakfast with their mom. Max and their dad had left for work several hours before. They were on the early shift, six in the morning until two in the afternoon.

"What a good idea," Tina Wilson remarked. She looked at the clock. "But could you two clean up the breakfast dishes for me before that, please?" she asked. "I don't want to be late for my first visit." The twins' mother worked in Ellandale and the surrounding towns as a nurse.

While Mrs. Wilson gathered her things together, Becky and Liam cleared the table. "So, no one can figure out how Monty escaped from the Reeds' yard?" she asked.

"No, and I suppose we'll never find out, either!" Liam grumbled.

"Let's just hope Monty doesn't do it again," Becky said.

"I still think Mrs. Reed must have let him out," Liam said suspiciously as he put away the place mats. "Then she got embarrassed when we showed up and she realized Dad was a policeman, so she pretended he'd escaped!"

"No, I don't think so," Becky said thoughtfully. "She really *did* look surprised to see Monty."

"Well, how *did* Monty get out, then?" Liam argued. "He didn't grow wings and fly over the gate, did he?"

Becky laughed.

"Okay, I'm off!" Mrs. Wilson said. "Mrs. Gibbs will take care of any problems while I'm gone. Dad will be back just after two o'clock." With that, she hurried out to her car.

Julie's mom, next door, had offered to keep an eye on Liam and Becky during the school vacation. Not that Liam and Becky thought they needed babysitting! But they were delighted that

Mrs. Gibbs had also offered to feed them lunch because, unlike their mom, she made great sandwiches!

The local pet store was called Fur, Fins, and Feathers and was run by a man named Mr. Burns. It was about halfway down the main street. Although the police supplied the Wilsons with everything Max needed, including food, Becky and Liam often visited the pet store to buy dog treats for him. They'd gotten to know Mr. Burns very well. He was a short, cheerful man, and although he loved all animals, he was particularly fond of dogs. He'd taken a real liking to Max.

"I suppose Monty could have dug a tunnel under the fence and escaped that way," Liam said as they reached the door of the pet store. "But Dad would have seen the hole, wouldn't he?"

"Will you stop talking about Monty?" Becky rolled her eyes and pushed her brother ahead of her into the store.

Liam opened his mouth to say something else but didn't get around to it once he saw who was already inside. Officer Wilson was standing, notebook and pencil in hand, talking to Mr. Burns. Max was sitting patiently at his side.

"Dad!" Liam exclaimed. "What are you doing here? *Ow!*" Becky had just elbowed him in the ribs.

"Sorry, Dad, we didn't mean to interrupt," she said. Then Becky gasped as she spotted two tiny kittens on the counter in front of Mr. Burns. They were adorable.

"Hello, you two," said Officer Wilson in a voice that warned them to remember that both he and Max were on duty.

Max remained seated by Officer Wilson. Although he adored Liam and Becky, he knew that Officer Wilson was his boss and that when they were on duty, he had to behave himself. Only Max's gently wagging tail showed that he recognized them.

"Hello, Liam, Becky. Meet Finbar and Lucy." Mr. Burns gently lifted the two kittens to say hello. "Someone left these two little monsters on my doorstep this morning. People can be so irresponsible! I'm trying to find a home for them. I don't suppose you'd be able to take them," he said, looking at Officer Wilson.

"I don't think so," the twins' father replied, smiling. "We've got enough on

our hands with Max to look after. But I'll ask around for you."

Mr. Burns smiled as the larger kitten, Finbar, scrambled up onto his shoulder. Then he turned back to Liam and Becky. "I was just telling your father about some shoplifting that's been going on here," the shopkeeper went on.

"What shoplifting?" Liam asked nosily. He moved quickly away from Becky before she could elbow him again. "Sorry, Dad," he muttered as his father frowned at him. "I was just interested."

Becky leaned forward and picked up the smaller kitten. It immediately started to purr like an engine.

"I don't mind you knowing," Mr. Burns said with a sigh. "Over the last couple of weeks I've had some of my stock stolen."

"What's been stolen?" Becky asked.

"Dog treats and dog toys, mostly," Mr. Burns told them.

Officer Wilson jotted something down in his notebook. "And you have absolutely no idea who's doing it?" he asked.

Mr. Burns shook his head. "None at all. I've never had a real problem with stealing before," he said miserably.

"Well, keep a close watch from now on," Officer Wilson advised the storekeeper. "Catching the thief red-handed is your best bet — and call us right away if you do. Don't try to tackle him yourself. I'll ask at some of the other stores to see if they've noticed an increase in shoplifting recently."

He smiled at Liam and Becky. "I'll see you two later," he said as he left the pet store. Max followed Officer Wilson obediently, not even glancing at the twins — or the kittens.

"Anyway, what can I get for you two?" Mr. Burns asked, trying to sound cheerful even though he was obviously worried.

"A bag of those yellow biscuits, please." Becky pointed to one of the large barrels of loose dog biscuits that were lined up in front of the shelves. She knew that the yellow ones were Scooter's favorite.

"I think this thief, whoever it is, is stealing my loose biscuits, too!" Mr. Burns complained as he reached for a paper bag. "I haven't sold as many biscuits as are missing from this barrel! The thieves must be filling their pockets with biscuits every time they come in!"

"Wouldn't you see them?" Liam asked.

"They're too clever for that!" Mr. Burns replied. He scooped some of the biscuits into the bag, weighed it, and handed it to Becky. "But next time, I'll be ready for them!"

Chapter Four

"Here you are, Scooter! Good boy!" Liam gave the little terrier his fourth biscuit in a row.

Scooter snapped it up and wolfed it down, licking his lips when he finished. Then he sat, staring longingly at the bag in Liam's hand as if he were starving.

"I think you've had enough, Scooter!" Julie said sternly. "Now fetch!" She flung the ball down the length of the Wilsons' yard, and Scooter charged after it.

It was after lunch, and Liam, Becky, and Julie had come over to play in the

Wilsons' yard because Julie's mom had hung laundry outside, and it got in the way of throwing the ball.

"Scooter seems to have recovered from yesterday," Becky remarked with a smile. The little terrier seemed back to normal and had been delighted with his bag of biscuits.

"It doesn't seem to have ruined his appetite, anyway!" Liam grinned as Scooter dropped the ball at Julie's feet and then pawed at Liam's leg, his gaze fixed on the biscuits.

"Nothing could do that!" replied Julie, throwing the ball again. This time Scooter trotted after it more reluctantly, casting a wistful look at the bag of biscuits as he went. "So who do you think the pet store thief is?" Julie asked. Liam and Becky had told Julie about meeting their dad and Max at the pet store earlier that morning.

"I have no idea," Becky replied. "But poor Mr. Burns seems really upset about it."

At that moment the back door opened, and Max trotted into the yard.

"Hi, Max!" Liam called as the German shepherd walked over to them, his long tail swishing back and forth. He looked pleased to be home after working all morning.

When Scooter spotted Max, he immediately lost interest in the ball and ran over to him. The two dogs sniffed each other in a friendly way, Scooter's stumpy little tail wagging like crazy.

"Max is Scooter's hero now!" Julie laughed as Liam gave both dogs a biscuit.

"Hello, kids." Officer Wilson followed Max out, a steaming cup of coffee in his hand. "How are things?"

"Dad, did you find the pet store thief?" Liam asked eagerly.

"Give me a chance!" His father made a face. "No, not yet. And I have to say, it's not very likely unless Mr. Burns catches someone in the act."

"Maybe you and Max should stake

out the store!" Liam suggested eagerly. "Becky and I could help!"

Officer Wilson laughed. "Thanks for the offer, but I'm afraid there are a few more serious crimes happening in the area than stealing dog treats! But you can help by keeping your eyes open when you're in Fur, Fins, and Feathers."

"We will," Becky promised.

"*And* we'll watch out for Monty, Dad," Liam said. "I bet his owners are letting him out on his own!"

Officer Wilson shook his head. "I have to say, I can't understand how else Monty got out of that garden," he admitted.

"Talking of dogs getting loose . . ." Tina Wilson, also carrying a cup of coffee, had come outside and overheard the conversation. She was still wearing her nurse's uniform because she'd just stopped home for a late lunch. "The same thing happened to one of my patients, Mrs. Chivers, this morning."

"What happened?" asked Liam, interested.

"Mrs. Chivers has a badly sprained wrist," the twins' mom explained, "and whenever I go to her house, we always put her West Highland white terrier, Hamish, outside in the yard because he runs off with the bandages!"

"And Hamish got out?" Liam asked.

Mrs. Wilson nodded. "He was only in the street behind the house, but I just couldn't understand how he got there. There was no way he could have escaped, as far as I could see."

"Just the same as Monty!" Becky exclaimed. "This is weird!"

"Did you tell the police, Mom?" Liam asked.

His mom shrugged. "I'm telling them now, aren't I?" she said, smiling at her husband. "No, there didn't seem to be much point. Hamish was found safe and sound, after all."

"Dad, do you think someone let Hamish and Monty out on purpose?" Becky asked.

Officer Wilson shook his head. "I have no idea, Becky. But why would someone do that?"

Chapter Five

"What are you two planning to do this afternoon?" Tina Wilson asked a couple of days later when she came home for a quick lunchtime sandwich.

"I'm going to the library," Becky said. Although Ellandale wasn't a big place, it had a library that was located in a converted house.

"I might go and see if some of the kids from school want to play a game of soccer in the park. And I might see if anyone would like a kitten while I'm there," Liam added.

Officer Wilson and Max had just arrived home from another early shift. Liam and Becky had quizzed their dad immediately about whether there had been any more mysterious "doggy incidents," but as far as Officer Wilson knew, there hadn't.

"Well, before you do," Mrs. Wilson produced a list from her pocket, "would you go shopping for me, please? I've got a couple of extra patients to visit, and by the time I've finished the supermarket will be closed."

"Oh, *Mom*!" Liam groaned.

But Becky took the list. "Okay, Mom," she agreed cheerfully. "Can we buy some candy if there's any money left over?"

Tina Wilson nodded her head and smiled. "All right!"

"Oh, cool!" Liam exclaimed. "Let's take Max, too."

"You know, I've been thinking about who could be letting these dogs loose," Becky remarked as they walked down the main street, Max trotting along beside them.

"And what do you think?" Liam asked eagerly.

"I don't have a clue!" Becky replied.

Liam made a face at her. "I really want to know. It's driving me crazy!"

Becky smothered a grin. Liam wasn't exactly the most patient person in the world! But her brother was right — it was a very frustrating mystery. There just didn't seem to be any answer to it.

"Maybe it's someone who doesn't like dogs," Liam suggested as they reached

Mason's, the small supermarket at the end of the street.

"But why would they let the dogs out?" Becky argued as she tied Max's leash to the bicycle rack just outside the supermarket door. "If this person, who-ever it is, doesn't like dogs, wouldn't he want to stay away from them?" She glanced at the German shepherd. "Sit, Max!"

Max, however, was sitting patiently on his haunches even before Becky got the words out. He was used to waiting and did so without any fuss at all.

Liam and Becky both gave him a pat and went inside. Becky grabbed a bas-ket on the way.

"Bread, sugar, flour, tea bags, lettuce, tomatoes," Becky muttered, gazing at the shopping list as they wandered down the first aisle.

"And don't forget the most important thing!" Liam reminded her. "Candy!"

Becky was reaching for lettuce from the fruit and vegetable display when suddenly she gasped, her eyes widening. "Liam! Look!"

"What?" Liam was filling a bag with tomatoes and wasn't paying much attention.

"There!" Becky yelled, pointing down the aisle. "It's a dog!"

Liam turned around and was just in time to see a small brown terrier dash right past him like a streak of lightning. The little dog stopped to sniff at some boxes stacked on the lower shelves, burrowing its nose in them until they all started toppling onto the floor. Then, with a little bark, it shot off again toward the delicatessen counter.

"Where did *it* come from?" Liam gasped, stepping over the fallen boxes of food.

"It just ran in through the door!" Becky replied. "I don't know where his owner is!"

Liam and Becky glanced at each other and knew immediately what the other was thinking. Was this another case of a dog being deliberately let loose?

Liam and Becky raced toward the deli counter. The terrier had its paws up on the cold cabinet, whimpering as it gazed longingly at the display of cold meats and cheeses.

The woman behind the counter was staring at the dog as if she couldn't believe her eyes. "No dogs allowed!" she snapped, glaring at Becky and Liam. "Is it yours?"

"No, it isn't!" Liam said indignantly.

Becky held out her hand to the terrier. "Good dog!" she said soothingly. "Come to Becky!"

The terrier stared at them with black, buttonlike eyes. For a moment it seemed as if the dog would obey, but then, tail wagging, it shot off again, past the twins and down the second aisle.

"It's obviously having too much fun to stop!" Liam gasped as they chased after it.

The dog had paused to grab a large box of pasta from one of the shelves, and it shook the box in its teeth as it ran. A moment later the box burst, and pasta shells flew all over the polished floor.

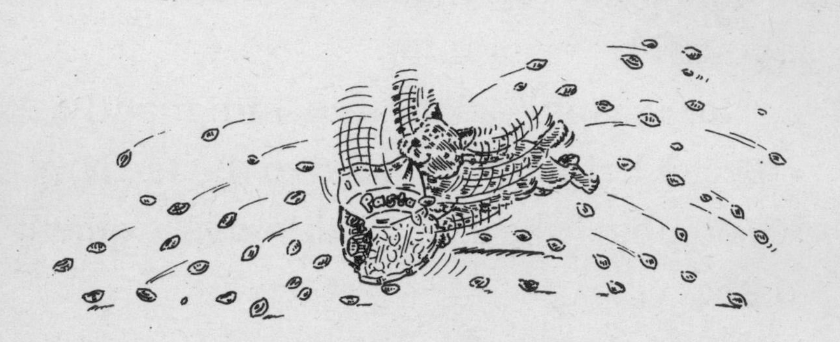

With a little bark, the terrier dropped the box and ran off, dodging an elderly woman who was pushing a shopping cart. The dog looked very pleased with itself.

"Hey, you!" A clerk in overalls who was stocking shelves at the other end of the aisle now came running toward the terrier. "Get that dog out of here!"

"That's what we're trying to do!" Liam

called back as he and Becky crunched their way through the pasta shells.

As the terrier stopped to sniff some packets of rice, a man in a suit, with a badge reading MANAGER: MR. SIMPKINS, and two women salesclerks also appeared at the other end of the aisle.

"This is disgraceful!" Mr. Simpkins spluttered, red in the face. "Disgraceful! Colin, catch that animal *immediately*!"

Colin, the stock clerk, moved cautiously toward the terrier, and Liam and Becky closed in on it, too, blocking the other end of the aisle.

The dog hesitated, realizing that both its exits were blocked. Barking, it ran over to the shelving display, wriggled under the gap at the bottom, and escaped into the next aisle.

Colin made a grab for the dog's

stumpy little tail as it disappeared, but he missed and ended up banging his head on the bottom shelf.

"It's getting away!" roared Mr. Simpkins furiously as he and his staff raced around the corner into the next aisle.

Liam and Becky were about to follow when Liam, out of the corner of his eye, saw something move. The terrier had doubled back and was heading for the first aisle again.

"Quick, Becky!" Liam grabbed her arm, and they turned back. But as they reached the beginning of the first aisle, the terrier was already racing toward the open door. In a moment or two it would be out in the street.

Becky thought fast. "MAX!" she yelled at the top of her voice. "MAX!"

The German shepherd immediately

leaped to his feet when he heard Becky's voice and strained toward the door as far as his leash would allow, to see what was going on.

The terrier stopped in its tracks, surprised to see such a big dog blocking its escape route. As Max stood his ground, eyeballing the smaller dog sternly, the terrier stayed where it was and began to whimper, uncertain what to do next.

Seconds later, Liam had scooped up the little dog and was holding it firmly. "Phew! At last!" he panted. "Nice job, Max!"

"Yes, nice job, Max!" Becky echoed gratefully. "You've saved the day again!"

Chapter Six

"And guess what, Dad?" Liam said breathlessly. "It was *exactly* the same as Monty and Hamish! The owner had left the dog —"

"Benjy," Becky added helpfully.

"Yeah, Benjy." Liam nodded. "Anyway, the owner had left Benjy in his yard and didn't have a clue how he'd gotten out!" He looked triumphantly at his father. "It's another doggy mystery!"

"It certainly sounds like it," Officer Wilson agreed.

Liam, Becky, and Max had just arrived

home with the groceries, and Liam immediately told their father what had happened.

"But how do you know all this?" Officer Wilson asked.

Liam grinned. "Because we waited while the supermarket manager, Mr. Simpkins, called the owner," he explained. "The dog had a tag on."

Officer Wilson laughed. "I suppose you two just couldn't tear yourselves away until you'd found out exactly what was going on! Didn't Mr. Simpkins mind?"

"No, because Liam was still holding the dog." Becky smiled. "I think Mr. Simpkins was a little scared of it!" She bent down and stroked Max, who was lying on the rug in front of the fireplace. "If it hadn't been for Max, we'd never have caught Benjy."

"So what are you going to *do*, Dad?" Liam asked impatiently. "You've got to solve this mystery!"

"Unfortunately, there's not a lot the police can do," Officer Wilson pointed out. "Unless an owner actually *sees* someone letting a dog out, we don't really have any hope of catching the person." He got up from his armchair when the doorbell rang. "That'll be Jim Thornton. I asked him to come over to discuss the Christmas concert."

"The what?" Becky asked as her father went over to the door.

Officer Wilson grinned. "I suggested that the Ellandale Police Station put on a Christmas concert this year!" he explained. "All proceeds go to charity."

"I bet Sergeant Thornton loved that!" Liam grinned. Sergeant Jim Thornton had worked at Ellandale Police Station for many years and was not exactly very open to new ideas. He still hadn't fully accepted Max as a member of his team.

Officer Wilson winked at them. "Oh, he'll get used to it!" he said and went out.

"Sounds like the police aren't going to do very much about the escaping dogs," Liam muttered to Becky.

"Well, you heard Dad," Becky pointed out sensibly. "There's not much they *can* do."

Liam nudged her. "No, but maybe *we* can!" he said.

Becky looked at him in surprise but didn't have a chance to say anything because Sergeant Thornton and their dad came in first.

"Hello, Sergeant Thornton," Liam said

eagerly. "So, what do *you* think about all these dogs that have been escaping?"

Jim Thornton, a middle-aged man with an almost permanently glum expression, sniffed and sat down as far away from Max as he could. Liam and Becky had thought at first that Sergeant Thornton didn't like animals at all. But then they'd discovered he had a cat named Inky that he thoroughly pampered!

"Very annoying!" Sergeant Thornton retorted. "The police don't have time to chase after dogs — *or* investigate disappearing dog treats!" He ignored Max as the dog walked toward him, expecting a greeting. "If people looked after their dogs, they wouldn't escape! We had another report this morning of a dog causing havoc on Lavender Street."

Liam and Becky sat up and looked at each other.

"I didn't hear about that, Jim," Officer Wilson said, also looking curious. "What happened?"

"There was an ice cream truck parked there, and the dog was jumping up at children, trying to steal their ice cream cones," Sergeant Thornton said. "It turned out the dog belonged to someone who lived just around the corner. The owner said the dog had been fenced in the yard, but obviously they'd let it out on its own and were too ashamed to say so!"

Liam nudged Becky. "Just like Monty, Hamish, and Benjy!"

"Okay, Jim, about this concert," said Officer Wilson cheerfully, and Sergeant Thornton looked even more glum.

Meanwhile, Liam and Becky went to the kitchen, and Max immediately followed them.

"What did you mean, maybe *we* can do something?" Becky asked as she raided the cookie jar.

"I think we should try to solve *both* mysteries ourselves!" Liam said. "After all, the police aren't going to do much, are they?" He ruffled Max's coat. Max looked up at Liam, his dark eyes curious. "And don't forget, we've got Max to help us, too!"

Liam, Becky, and Max were on their way to Fur, Fins, and Feathers.

"I don't see how we're going to find out who's letting the dogs loose," Becky said. "Not unless we actually see them do it."

"Okay, maybe we don't have much hope of solving *that* mystery," Liam admitted reluctantly. "But I bet we can find out who the pet store thief is! All we have to do is hang around for a while and see who goes in and out."

"All right." Becky shrugged. She didn't think it would be that simple, but she was prepared to give it a try.

When they reached the pet store, a woman pushing a baby in a stroller was trying to hold the door open and get the stroller out at the same time. Mr. Burns was busy serving another customer and hadn't noticed that the woman was having problems.

Liam politely jumped forward and held the door. The woman smiled at him. "Thank you," she said. "Say thank you, Megan!"

Becky and Liam hadn't noticed that the woman had another child, who was behind her. She was a fair-haired, red-cheeked little girl of about four, wearing a bright blue scarf and matching hat.

"Thank you!" Megan lisped and gave Liam and Becky a mischievous grin. Then she spotted Max, and her eyes lit up. "Mommy, look at the dog!" she exclaimed.

"Now, Megan, we don't have time to stop and pet every dog we meet!" her mom said hastily, ushering the little girl along the street.

Liam and Becky couldn't help smiling as Megan pouted crossly.

"Hi, Mr. Burns," Liam said eagerly as soon as the last customer had left. "We've come to buy some dog treats for Max. What's been happening? Do you

still have the kittens? Has anything else been stolen?"

The pet store owner nodded as he came from behind the counter to pet Max. "The kittens are at home, being spoiled rotten by my wife. But things aren't so good in the store. We've had something stolen almost every day," he said gloomily. Then he groaned and pointed to one of his shelves. "And something else has disappeared since this morning! I had one bag of K9 Dog Chews left, and now it's gone!"

"Are you *sure* you didn't sell it?" Becky asked.

Mr. Burns nodded his head. "Certain. I remember seeing it when I opened the store and thinking it was time I ordered some more."

"Do you know when it disappeared?" Liam asked.

Mr. Burns frowned. "I *think* it was there when I closed for lunch, but I'm not sure."

"Well, at least we know the thief came in today sometime!" Liam exclaimed, excited. They were onto something now! "Can you remember all your customers so far, Mr. Burns?"

"Well . . ." Mr. Burns scratched his

head. "I don't know all their names, of course. But there was Mrs. Adams, and Mr. Nixon —"

Becky interrupted him. She was staring at Max, who was sniffing something on the ground and pawing it with interest.

"What is it, Max?" Becky asked.

"Maybe it's a clue!" Liam gasped, his face lighting up.

Chapter Seven

Becky and Liam both rushed over excitedly — until they saw what Max was sniffing at. It was a child's bright blue glove.

"Is that all?" Liam asked in disgust. "Honestly, Max, I thought you'd found something interesting!"

"I think it might belong to that little girl, Megan." Becky frowned as she remembered what the little girl had been wearing. "This glove's exactly the same color as her scarf and hat. It must be part of a matching set."

"Oh, you mean Mrs. Collins's little girl," Mr. Burns said, giving Max a dog biscuit from one of the barrels. "They're a very nice family. Mrs. Collins is always doing errands for the elderly people in the neighborhood where they live. A lot of them have pets, so she comes in here almost every day to pick up things for them."

Liam was still feeling disappointed. "I

really thought we had a breakthrough there!" he muttered.

"Maybe we should go after them and return the glove," Becky suggested. "It looks pretty new."

"But I thought we were going to stay here and try to figure out who the thief could be," Liam objected.

"It won't take more than a couple of minutes," Becky pointed out. "They can't be far from here. Besides, that would give Mr. Burns time to make a list of all the customers who've been in today. I'm sure Dad would like to see it."

"That's a very good idea, Becky." Mr. Burns was already reaching for a pen and notepad. "I'll do it right away."

"See?" Liam said triumphantly as they went out of the store. "I told you we'd solve the pet store thief mystery!"

"We haven't yet," Becky reminded him. "But at least we've narrowed down the list of suspects! Now, which way did Megan and her mom go?"

"That way." Liam pointed to the other end of the main street, the opposite of the way they'd come. "I can't see them, though."

"Maybe they're in one of the other stores," Becky suggested. She, Liam, and Max hurried along the street, glancing into each of the stores, but there was no sign of the Collins family.

At the end of the main street, the road branched off in several directions. They spotted Megan and her mom walking down Lilac Hill, which led to the new housing development. Mrs. Collins had obviously met someone she knew, because she was chatting with an elderly woman and walking slowly so that her friend could keep up. Megan was trailing behind, walking even slower. She had a stick in her hand and was dragging it along a set of railings.

"Look!" Becky nudged Liam. Megan was wearing one blue glove on the hand that held the stick. "It must be hers!"

"Well, I suppose that's one mystery solved," Liam said. "Let's run and catch up with them. I'm dying to get back to the store and see Mr. Burns's list of suspects!"

"Why, what are you going to do?" Becky teased as they all broke into a run, Max included. "Raid all the customers' houses to find out if they've got piles of stolen dog biscuits in their kitchen cabinets?"

"No, but Dad and Max can!" Liam said

with a grin. "Max would sniff them out in no time, wouldn't you, boy?"

Max gave a short, sharp bark as he loped down the hill alongside Liam and Becky, easily keeping pace with them.

"Max would sniff dog biscuits from a mile away!" Becky joked.

They were still far behind the Collins family when Becky suddenly skidded to a halt and grabbed Liam's arm. "Look, Liam!" She pointed down Lilac Hill. "What on earth is Megan doing?"

Chapter Eight

Liam and Becky both stopped and stared. Megan was behaving very oddly. The little girl had stopped beside the front gate of one of the houses on Lilac Hill and was trying to open it.

"They don't live there, do they?" Liam muttered, puzzled.

Becky shook her head. "No, Mr. Burns said they live in the new housing development."

They both watched Megan struggle with the gate latch. She was frowning hard as she concentrated on what she was doing, but even when she used both hands to try to lift the latch, it was still too stiff for her little fingers.

"Come on," Liam said impatiently. "Let's give Mrs. Collins Megan's glove and get back to the pet store."

"No, wait." Becky clutched his arm. "What's she doing *now*?"

Megan had stopped trying to unlatch the gate. Her mom was still deep in conversation with her friend and hadn't realized that Megan was so far behind them. The little girl put her hand into her pocket and pulled something out. Liam and Becky were too far away to see what it was.

"What *is* she up to?" Liam muttered.

Megan reached down and passed whatever she had taken out of her pocket through the bars of the gate.

Then she stood up, just as her mom turned around to see where she was.

"Megan!" Mrs. Collins called, sounding rather irritated. "Keep up, sweetheart."

Megan immediately scampered off, leaving Liam and Becky more puzzled than ever.

"What on earth did she put through that gate?" Becky asked, wide-eyed.

"Let's go and check it out!" Liam suggested.

They hurried down the hill toward the gate where Megan had stopped.

"There's nothing here!" Becky said as she stared into the empty yard.

"Wait a minute, Becky," Liam said, looking down at Max. The German shepherd was straining toward the gate, sniffing the air, all of his highly developed senses on alert. "Max can smell something!"

Max gave a bark, almost as if he was telling Liam he was right. And a few seconds later a woolly-looking black poodle trotted out from behind a large bush. It had the remains of a dog treat in its mouth and was crunching the last bite enthusiastically. It spotted Max and rushed over to the gate, giving a welcoming bark as the two dogs sniffed each other cautiously through the bars.

"Megan must have given the dog that treat," Becky said. "And she tried to let it out!"

Liam nodded. "Hang onto that glove for now, Becky," he said. "I think we should follow Megan and see what else she's doing!"

Becky agreed, so she, Liam, and Max set off again, keeping far behind Megan.

Nothing happened until they reached the bottom of Lilac Hill. Mrs. Collins was still walking with her friend and hadn't noticed that her daughter was trailing behind again. Then Megan stopped outside another gate.

"Look!" Liam nudged Becky. "She's going to do it again!"

Liam and Becky moved closer but

stayed on the other side of the street so that Megan wouldn't notice them. This time, they had a clear view of the gate. A shaggy red-haired mutt was on the other side, its tail wagging like crazy.

"Hello, doggy!" they heard Megan say. "Do you want to go to the park?" She began to fiddle with the gate latch.

"Do you think we should stop her?" Becky asked in a worried voice.

Liam nodded. But it was already too late. Just as Liam, Becky, and Max went to stop her, Megan pushed open the gate, and the dog trotted out. The little girl grinned, put her hand in her pocket, and gave the dog a treat.

A second later her mom turned around to see where the little girl was, after saying good-bye to her friend.

"Megan!" Mrs. Collins called anxiously when she saw her daughter standing beside the dog. "Haven't I told you not to pet dogs you don't know? It's very dangerous! Now come here and hold my hand!"

Megan ran off reluctantly, leaving the dog standing on the sidewalk.

Liam nudged Becky. "I think we've solved the mystery of the escaping

dogs!" he said. "It must be Megan who's letting them out!"

"We'd better tell the dog's owner that he's loose," Becky pointed out. Then she gasped in horror. "Oh, no!"

While they'd been watching Megan, the dog had run out into the middle of the road. A car was speeding along, heading straight for it.

Chapter Nine

The young woman driver had spotted the dog and had slammed on her brakes, but it was too late. There was no way the car could stop in time, and the dog was cowering in its path, frozen with fear.

Then Max barked sharply.

The sound seemed to bring the dog to its senses. It sprang to life and dashed toward Max just seconds before the car passed them and skidded to a stop farther down the street.

Liam immediately grabbed the dog's collar and pulled it off the road.

"Good boy, Max!" Becky said in a shaky voice, dropping to her knees and burying her face in Max's thick fur.

Max licked her cheek, his tail swishing gently from side to side.

Meanwhile, several things were happening all at once. The car's driver rushed over to check that the dog was all

right. The sound of the near accident had made Megan and her mom turn around. And seeing the dog almost hit by the car made the little girl burst into tears.

At the same time, the dog's owner had rushed out of her kitchen to see what was going on. "Bobby!" she cried, hurrying out into the street to claim her pet. "How on earth did you get out?"

"Your gate must have been open," Becky said quickly, with a glance at Liam. They didn't want to get Megan into trouble, although they would certainly have to tell her mom what had been going on. "But it's okay, it was a near miss."

Reassured, the driver got back into her car and drove off.

Looking rather shaken, Bobby's

owner scooped him up and took him back into the yard. Meanwhile, Liam, Becky, and Max hurried over to Mrs. Collins and Megan, who was still sobbing.

"Megan, what's the matter, darling?" Mrs. Collins asked, puzzled, as she wiped her daughter's face with a tissue.

"It was me who let the doggy out!" Megan hiccuped between sobs. "But I didn't want it to get hurt!"

"Megan, what are you talking about?" Mrs. Collins looked completely mystified.

"Hello, Mrs. Collins," Liam said awkwardly as he, Becky, and Max went up to them. It was hard to know what to say.

Megan's mom looked at them for a moment, then smiled. "Oh, you were at the pet store a minute ago, weren't you?" she said. "Aren't you Officer Wilson's children?"

Liam and Becky nodded, and then Becky took the plunge. "Mrs. Collins, we followed you to give this back to you." She took Megan's glove from her pocket and handed it over. "But there's something else we think you should know."

Megan's mom listened in silence as Liam and Becky explained how someone had been letting dogs loose around Ellandale for the last few days. Then she frowned. "You think it was *Megan*?"

"Well, we saw her let Bobby out," Liam replied. "And she tried to let another dog out before, too."

Mrs. Collins bent down so she could look at her daughter. "Megan," she said gently, "have you been opening people's gates and letting their dogs out?"

There was a moment's silence, and then the little girl nodded. "They wanted to go to the park and play with all the other dogs and have fun," she explained. "So I let them out."

Mrs. Collins shook her head. "Oh, Megan!" She sighed. "That was a very naughty thing to do! Dogs shouldn't be out on their own. They might get lost or hurt. You saw what almost happened just now, didn't you?"

Megan's lower lip began to wobble again. "I didn't mean for the doggy to get run over!" she whimpered.

"Well, I suppose there's no real harm done." Mrs. Collins gave the little girl a hug. "But you must promise never to do it again, Megan!"

"I promise!" Megan mumbled tearfully.

"Actually, there's something else," Becky said quietly. "I think you'd better ask Megan what she has in her pockets!"

Chapter Ten

"What?" Megan's mom could hardly believe her ears, and even Liam looked at Becky in confusion. What was his twin sister talking about?

Looking rather sheepish, Megan was already emptying out her pockets. There was an open bag of K9 Dog Chews in one of them, and the other was stuffed with loose dog biscuits from one of Mr. Burns's barrels.

"Of course!" Liam exclaimed as he put two and two together. "Megan is the pet store thief! That's where she got the treats to feed the dogs!" He grinned at Becky. "Nice one, Becky!"

"Megan!" Mrs. Collins had turned very pale. "What *have* you been up to? Have you been taking things from the pet store?"

"I only wanted a few treats to give to the nice doggies," Megan muttered. "And Mr. Burns has *lots* of dog biscuits!"

"Oh, Megan!" Mrs. Collins wailed.

"I've told you before not to take things that don't belong to you!" She looked at Liam and Becky. "Oh, dear, this is all very embarrassing! What am I going to say to Mr. Burns? He told me about the thief, but I never dreamed it was Megan!"

"Mr. Burns is so nice, I'm sure he won't mind when he finds out the truth, Mrs. Collins," Becky said consolingly.

"Do you think so?" Mrs. Collins asked. "I think I'd better go and see him right away to explain. Maybe you could come, too."

Liam and Becky agreed, so they all retraced their steps and headed back to the main street. Megan was very quiet and subdued at first, but she began to cheer up when Becky and Liam let her pet Max.

"Megan loves animals," Mrs. Collins confided in Liam and Becky as they walked up the main street. "I suppose that's why all this happened!"

"Does Megan have a pet of her own?" Becky asked.

"Not yet," Mrs. Collins replied, "although I've promised her a puppy or kitten when she gets older." She grinned ruefully. "Maybe I'll have to get her one sooner rather than later!"

Becky caught Liam's eye. She knew he was thinking about Mr. Burns's kittens. But the idea was just too good to be true — they'd never persuade Mrs. Collins to adopt both Finbar and Lucy. Or maybe they could . . .

They reached the pet store and went in. Becky felt sorry for Megan's mom, who was looking very nervous.

"Oh, hello!" There was no one in the store except Mr. Burns, who looked very surprised to see them all. "I'll be with you in just a second, Mrs. Collins. Liam and Becky, I've made this list of the people who've been in the store today. Could you pass it on to your dad?"

"I don't think we'll need to, Mr. Burns," Liam said. "You see, we know who's been stealing from your store!"

"I'm very sorry, Mr. Burns," Mrs. Collins added, "but I'm afraid it was Megan!"

"Megan!" the pet store owner repeated in an amazed voice as Megan turned pink and disappeared behind her mom.

Mrs. Collins quickly explained what had happened, with a little help from

Liam and Becky, and Mr. Burns listened in silence.

"Well!" he said with a smile when they'd finished. "So Megan's the one I've been looking for all this time! I never suspected a thing!"

"I'm terribly sorry, Mr. Burns," said Mrs. Collins. "Of course, I'll pay you for anything Megan took."

Mr. Burns shook his head. "Let's just forget about it, okay?" he said generously. "After all, you're one of my best customers, Mrs. Collins!"

"That's very kind of you." Mrs. Collins looked relieved. Then she glanced at Megan, who'd crept out from her hiding place to give Max a pat. "And Megan, you must *never* take anything from Mr. Burns's store again. In fact, you must not take *anything* that doesn't belong to you without asking first. Do you understand?"

Megan nodded sheepishly.

Liam and Becky glanced at each other and grinned. With Max's help, they'd done exactly what they'd set out to do — they'd solved *both* of Ellandale's doggy mysteries in one afternoon. Now they couldn't wait to tell their dad! There was just one more problem to solve.

"Oh, by the way, Mrs. Collins," Liam said innocently. "Did you know that Mr. Burns has two kittens he's trying to find a nice home for?"

"Maybe you should give me and Becky a job at the Ellandale Police Station, Dad," Liam remarked as he opened a can of soda.

Officer Wilson laughed. "I have to hand it to you two," he said, raising his eyebrows as he set the kitchen table. "You certainly managed to put one over on the police this time!"

"Yes, good job!" the twins' mother chimed in. She was standing by the stove, making spaghetti for dinner. "You managed to solve two mysteries at the same time!"

"And the best news is, we've helped Finbar and Lucy find a home," Becky said. "Megan and her mom are going to adopt them!"

"Well, I knew we could do it!" Liam said with absolutely no modesty at all. "As soon as we saw Megan letting the dogs out *and* feeding them treats, it was a piece of cake!"

"Hey, you!" Becky gave her brother a

shove. "It was *me* who put two and two together and guessed that Megan was also the pet store thief!"

"Well, I think you're both very smart," their mother said, adding a generous handful of spaghetti to the pot full of boiling water. "I still don't understand what made you suspect Megan, though."

"Yes, tell us again what happened," said Officer Wilson. He reached under the table, where Max was lying quietly, and scratched the German shepherd's ears. "Why did you start following Megan in the first place?"

Liam and Becky looked at each other and grinned.

"Well, actually, it was because of the glove that Max found in the pet store," Liam admitted.

Knowing he was being talked about,

Max walked out from under the table and stretched himself, yawning.

"If it hadn't been for Max, we'd never have gone after Megan and we'd never have found out what she was doing," Becky added.

"Oh, so it's *Max* who's the real hero!" Officer Wilson said teasingly.

"Yes, he is," Becky agreed. She reached out to pet Max, who gave a little bark of acknowledgment and looked remarkably pleased with himself.

"Fair enough, Max," Liam said with a grin. "Yes — it was *you* who solved the pet store job."